My name is RJ,
and I just
don't like the
sound of the word

NO!

It seems like everybody always tells me **NO**.

NO RJ this, **NO** RJ that...

Sometimes I think my real name is **NO RJ!**

I Just Don't Like the Sound of NO!

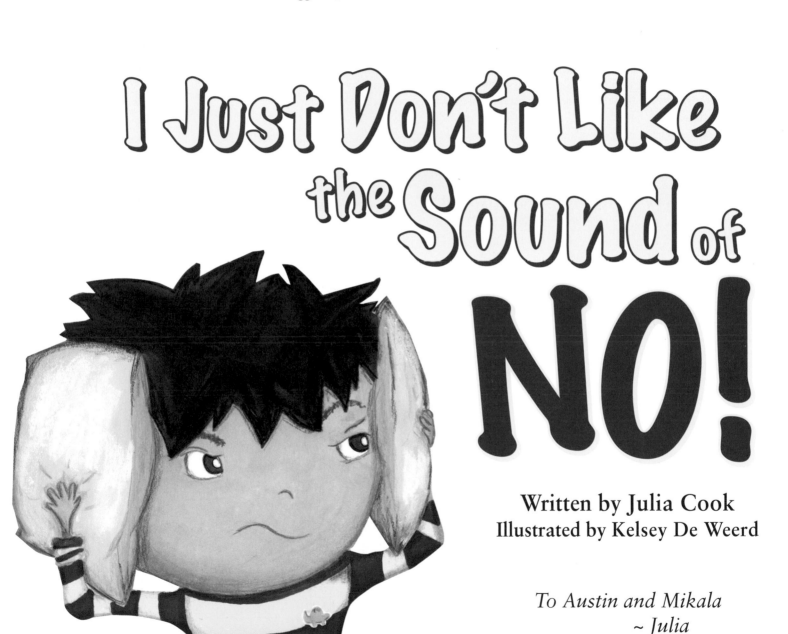

Written by Julia Cook
Illustrated by Kelsey De Weerd

To Austin and Mikala
~ Julia

BOYS TOWN
Press

Boys Town, Nebraska

I Just Don't Like the Sound of NO!
Text and Illustrations Copyright © 2011 by Father Flanagan's Boys' Home
ISBN 978-1-934490-25-9

Published by the Boys Town Press
13603 Flanagan Blvd.
Boys Town, NE 68010

For a Boys Town Press catalog, call **1-800-282-6657**
or visit our website: **boystownpress.org**

Publisher's Cataloging-in-Publication Data

Cook, Julia, 1964-

I just don't like the sound of NO! : my story about accepting 'no' for an answer and disagreeing ... the right way! / written by Julia Cook ; illustrated by Kelsey De Weerd. -- Boys Town, NE : Boys Town Press, c2011.

p. ; cm.
(Best me I can be)

ISBN: 978-1-934490-25-9
Audience: grades K-6.
Summary: Shows readers the steps to the fundamental social skills of accepting "no" and disagreeing appropriately. When RJ learns to use these skills the right way, he finds that rewards come his way, instead of arguments.

1. Children--Life skills guides--Juvenile fiction. 2. Obedience--Juvenile fiction. 3. Conflict (Psychology)--Juvenile fiction. 4. Interpersonal communication--Juvenile fiction. 5. Frustration--Juvenile fiction. 6. [Obedience--Fiction. 7. Conflict (Psychology)--Fiction. 8. Interpersonal communication--Fiction. 9. Frustration--Fiction.] I. De Weerd, Kelsey. II. Series: Best me I can be (Boys Town).

PZ7.C76984 I15 2011

E   1108

Printed in the United States
15 14 13 12 11

Boys Town Press is the publishing division of Boys Town, a national organization serving children and families.

A few days ago, I was at the store with my dad. I saw a box of smelly markers that I really, really wanted.

"Dad," I asked. "Can you buy these for me?"

"No," he said.

"But I just don't like the sound of NO, how about **maybe?**"

"No!" he said. "Not today."

"But I just don't like the sound of NO, how about **we'll see?**"

"No!" he said. "Remember RJ, I told you before we left home,
this trip to the store is a looking trip for you not a buying trip."

"But, Dad, they have one that smells like bubble gum!
There's cherry and banana and..."

"RJ... No means NO!"

When we got home, my best friend Sam asked me if I wanted
to sleep over at his house.

"Mom, can Sam and I have a sleepover tonight?"

"No," my mom said, "not tonight."

"But I just don't like the sound of NO, how about **I'll think about it?**"

"No," my mom said. "You can't have a sleepover on a school night.
You won't get enough rest and then you'll be tired tomorrow at school."

8

The next day at school, I asked my teacher,
"Can we have extra free time?"

"No, RJ," she said, "not today."

"I just don't like the sound of NO, how about maybe **later?**"

"No RJ. Today we have a full schedule and we just can't fit it in."

"But I just don't like the sound of NO, how about **after lunch?**"

"No, RJ. I told you NOT today."

"But last week you said..."

"No means NO! RJ, you need to learn how to accept 'No' for an answer."

LOOK WHAT'S NEW!

HOW TO JOIN THE
SAY YES TO NO CLUB

☑ Accepting NO for an Answer

☑ Disagreeing the Right Way

"I think you need to try to become a member
of the Say YES to NO Club."

"How do I do that?" I asked.

"Well, to join, you have to be able to do two things:
Accept 'No' for an answer and learn how to disagree appropriately."

LOOK right at the person who is telling you 'No.'

Say **'OKAY'** to the person, he's running the show.

STAY CALM on the inside and don't disagree.

You can **ASK** him why later, this is how you should be.

"To disagree with someone the right way,
here is what you should do:

LOOK right at the person
when you disagree.

Don't scream or use mean
words, be the BEST you can be.

Tell why you feel
differently, give your
REASONS with facts.

LISTEN closely to what she
says, this is how you should act.

"RJ, if you can learn how to do these two things, you can become an official member of the Say YES to NO Club!

Then you will get to write your name on a star and put it up on our Say YES to NO Star Board.

Once your star is up on the board, your name will be put into a weekly drawing and you could even win a prize!"

"Do I have to do it at home too?" I asked.

"Absolutely! In order to become an official member, your parents have to sign a paper saying that you are being a Say YES to NO expert at home too."

I looked at the **Say YES to NO** Star Board. It would be pretty cool to see my name up there on one of those stars, and the prizes my teacher gives away are awesome!

Margaret Ann walked by and overheard me talking to my teacher.

"Being a member of the **Say YES to NO** Club is fun, RJ," she said.

"You get to decorate your star any way you want to."

"Okay," I told my teacher,

"I'll do it!"

After lunch, I asked my teacher, "Can we have extra recess today?"

"No!" she replied.

It wasn't easy, but I looked up at her and I said, **"Okay."**

"Thanks for accepting 'No,' RJ," she said and gave me a thumbs up.

Then I went back
to my seat.

That night, I was at home getting
    some ice cream out of our freezer
when my mom said,

"No, RJ, you can't eat that now."

21

In my head, I was thinking, "I just don't like the sound of NO, and besides I'm STARVING!"

But, then I thought about how my name would look on one of those stars...

"Okay, Mom, I'll put it back."

My mom looked at me like she was in shock!

I could have knocked her over with a feather!

"Thank you, RJ," she said. And then she gave me a great big hug.

24

Before I went to bed,
I asked my mom,

"Why wouldn't you let me eat ice cream tonight?
I was so hungry!"

"Well, RJ, you wanted
    ice cream right before dinner and I
didn't want you to spoil
        your appetite."

    "Oh," I said.

"I am so proud of you, RJ.

Even when you disagreed with me, you waited to talk to me about it until you were calm, and then you didn't argue!"

Last week I earned my star, and my name got put
into the Say YES to NO special drawing.

Today, my teacher picked a name, and guess who won?

28

I DID!

My awesome prize was
a box of smelly markers,
just like the ones I wanted
my dad to buy me at the store!

Becoming a Say YES to NO expert
really paid off for me.

Today was one of the
BEST days of my life **EVER!**